THE LOST SAILOR

by Pam Conrad

illustrated by Richard Egielski

A Laura Geringer Book   *An Imprint of HarperCollinsPublishers*

The Lost Sailor
Text copyright © 1992 by Pam Conrad
Illustrations copyright © 1992 by Richard Egielski
Printed in the U.S.A. All rights reserved.
Typography by Al Cetta
1   2   3   4   5   6   7   8   9   10
First Edition

Library of Congress Cataloging-in-Publication Data
Conrad, Pam.
    The lost sailor / by Pam Conrad ; illustrated by Richard Egielski.
        p.   cm.
    "A Laura Geringer book."
    Summary: A sailor famed for his seamanship and luck is shipwrecked on a
tiny island, where his darkest hour gives rise to rescue and a new life.
    ISBN 0-06-021695-6. — ISBN 0-06-021696-4 (lib. bdg.)
    [1. Shipwrecks—Fiction.   2. Sea stories.]   I. Egielski, Richard, ill.   II.
Title.
PZ7.C76476Lo   1992   91-39640
[E]—dc20   CIP
                                                                  AC

For Nadine
—P.C.

For my son, Ian
—R.E.

ONCE UPON A SEA, on a place on the earth where sailors travel for days on end without ever seeing a rock or a bird or the smallest blade of grass, there traveled a sailor aboard a ship called the *Promise*. This sailor was known from longitude to longitude, from latitude to latitude, for his great seamanship and incredible luck.

At his touch, the halyards and lines would send the sails to breathtaking heights and set his glorious ship on a tilt with such speed and grace that the very air about her hummed with balance.

This sailor could spin around five times blindfolded, stop, and point dead north with his finger every time. And when there was a fog, he would close his eyes and steer through the thickness by instinct, by the feel of the air on the hairs of his arms and the breath of the ocean in his nose.

He could tell the weather from miles off and predict a puff of wind within millionths of a second. "A storm will hit us in eighteen hours," he'd tell his crew, and after seventeen hours, they would gather up their playing cards and laundry and prepare the *Promise* for rough seas.

This sailor always steered the bow of the *Promise* into the swells, had never seen her mast crack or his charts crumple. When the winds died and there was nothing to do, he would entertain his crew by tying knots with his toes.

He was a gifted sailor. And a lucky man.

Then one cold afternoon when looking up into the sky was like looking into a cauldron of bubbling, boiling bean soup, the sailor stood at the helm of the *Promise* and held very still. His crew wrung their hands and prepared for a storm. They emptied their coffee cups and reefed the sails. They secured the lifeboats and tuned the shrouds.

"Quite a storm, eh, captain?" they called.

"It will hit any minute, don't you think?"

But he said not a word.

The crew stood by at their posts and waited for orders, while the sea churned and lightning cracked in the cauldron of the skies. "I have never seen it quite like this," the sailor whispered. Suddenly the crew saw him grip the wheel and flatten his feet firm and wide against the deck. At that instant a blast of wind hit the *Promise* as she had never been hit before.

Again and again the sailor turned her bow into the wind and the rain, into the fierce breaking waves. The mainmast of the *Promise* bent like a willow, and her sails strained till they tore to shreds and blew like telltales.

The sailor saw his men thrown overboard, kicking and yelling, and he saw his lifeboats fly like gulls and explode into splinters in the air. He watched as the towering mast cracked like a wooden match. Then suddenly the ship's wheel broke from its hold, and with the sailor still gripping it for dear life, it flew across the deck, over the side, and plunged into the sea.

The sailor watched through the breaking waves as he drifted away from the *Promise*. She rose and dove, and before his eyes she was twisted and bent in ways he had never seen a ship twist and bend before. *"My Promise! My Promise!"* he wept. And then she groaned like death. Her hull blew wide open, and before his very eyes, she went down.

All was lost.

The lost sailor's torn jacket was tangled in the spokes of the *Promise*'s wheel, and in this way he floated for three days and three nights through the storm. He floated near death, benumbed by cold and delirious with grief.

Until one morning the sun cracked the seam of the horizon, and there was birdsong in the air. The sailor lay still across the spokes of the wheel, no longer tossing about, and when the sun had warmed his back, he opened his eyes and watched the sandpipers running up and down the beach.

"I'm alive," he said, and he stood and looked about.

He saw that he was on the smallest of islands, surrounded by the sea. The only sound was the pounding of the waves on the shore. And the birds. Gulls flew out over the waves, and looking beyond them, he saw nothing. No other ship dotted the horizon. No other sailor had been washed up on the shore. The lost sailor was alone.

Dazed and bedraggled, he stumbled after the sandpipers as they followed the gentle ebb and flow of the waves. Seashells dotted the sand, hunks of coral lay half buried, starfish and sand dollars lay pulsing in the sun. Then there at his feet, in its wooden box, was his sextant, washed ashore! He picked it up and walked on. And there! One of the sails still in its bag. And a coffee cup. A couple of charts rolled in their cases. And a lantern, unbroken but full of water. The sailor walked along gathering up what he could and storing them in the sail bag.

Then he waited and waited to be rescued. He sat on the beach all day long with his sail bag, waiting. But day after day the horizon was empty.

The sailor wondered if he would ever sail again. Would he ever feel the pitch and the roll of the ocean beneath his feet? Would he again feel the cool spray across his brow? Or watch the green glow of his churning wake? The sailor's eyes filled with tears. Oh, to steer by a star, to swim in the shadow of his anchored *Promise*. But already the rocking in his ears had ceased. Everything was still.

All was lost.

When the sailor grew tired of sleeping on the beach, and hungry for more than just clams and seaweed, he ventured deep into the island, dragging his sail bag behind him. It wasn't a bad island. There were some fruit trees, a freshwater pond, and a fine view of the westerly path of clouds and stars. So he spilled out his sail bag, and from the few things he had left, the lost sailor built a home for himself among the palm trees.

And there he waited for years and years.

Each day he would gather kiwis for his dinner. He squeezed palm leaves to make oil for his lantern. He made his soft bed of coconut fuzz and sailcloth and added another notch on a nearby tree for each day spent alone. Then, when his chores were through, he would sit on the beach and wait to be rescued.

The lost sailor built sand castles. He got a tan. He buried himself. He collected shells and beach glass, and every day he searched the bare horizon for the sight of an arriving ship.

At night he would sit and try to figure out where he was. The lamplight was dim, but he would pore over his charts, checking every drop of charted seas. But even allowing for variance and deviance and current and forgetfulness, his island was nowhere on the charts. No matter how hard he looked. Year after year.

Then one night, he searched longer than usual, till he was bone weary and nodding over the charts. "I will never be found," he finally sighed. And in his sadness he forgot to blow out his lantern, and he forgot to roll up his chart. He walked outside to watch the moon glittering a path on the sea.

Suddenly there was a noise behind him—the sound of an old sea chart coiling itself up with a snap, and then the sound of a lantern falling on its side. The lost sailor turned, but he was too late. The palm-leaf roof went up like firecrackers. The old sailcloth blazed a fierce orange, and when it was gone, the coconut fuzz burned purple and smoked. The lost sailor ran in circles around his hut, crying, "Oh no! This is all I had left!" But the fire paid him no mind. It roared and burned and crackled until nothing was left. Nothing was left. Even the sextant had melted down to a lump of sandy metal.

The sailor stood beside the smoldering, smoking heap. Now truly, all was lost. Turning away from the ruins, he stumbled down to the beach and threw himself on the very spot where he had washed ashore years before.

"All is lost," he cried. "All is lost." And he fell into a troubled sleep on the sand.

The sun warmed him the next morning, and he lifted his head. The gulls and sandpipers were still there. When he looked out to the horizon, he gasped. He jumped up. He ran back and forth wa-hooping and shouting, for there, in the water, coming closer and closer, was a man rowing a small wooden dinghy. But better than that—even better than that!—was the huge sailing ship on the horizon with its sails furled and its anchor lines out.

"Ahoy!" the rowing man called, coming closer and closer.

"Ahoy!" the found sailor answered. He was dancing and leaping on the sand, and when the dinghy was close enough, he splashed out to meet it. The rowing man pulled him aboard and turned the dinghy about. The found sailor sat grinning in amazement. "I thought all was lost," he told the rowing man. "Last night I lost everything, all that was left of the *Promise*."

The rowing man kept rowing. "I don't know about that, Captain," he said. "All I know is that it's a good thing you lit that fire last night."

The found sailor sat very still. "The fire?"

"Yes, sir. If you hadn't lit that fire, we would've sailed right on by. We never would've known this island was here."

The morning sun shone so brightly, the found sailor could barely look at the water. He squinted into the glare and watched until the mighty sailing ship loomed above him. The crew sent down a rope ladder, and when he climbed up, the man in the dinghy called out, "It's the captain of the *Promise*!"

The crew applauded and saluted him, calling among themselves, "Look! It's that famous sailor! Known from longitude to longitude, from latitude to latitude. The captain of the *Promise*!"

The captain of this new ship was waiting on the deck to meet the found sailor. Their eyes met as they shook hands. "I have heard many things about you," the captain said. "It is said you are a gifted sailor."

The sailor smiled. He had not forgotten how to steady himself aboard a gently rolling deck, and when he shaded his eyes and looked up at the tall mast, he saw a dozen sandpipers circling its tip.

"A gifted sailor," he agreed. "A gifted sailor and a lucky man."